THE LOOK

DIANE NARRAWAY
AN UNUSUAL ROMANCE

Text © Diane Narraway
Edited by Bekki Milner
Cover image by Alexey Klen.

ISBN: 978-1-916756-18-2
Veneficia Publications
February 2024

VENEFICIA PUBLICATIONS UK
veneficiapublications.com

For Marian

CONTENTS

FOREWORD
Marisha Kiddle

Many years ago, I started researching my family tree. My mother's side became quite difficult as she had never met her grandparents from her father's side. We heard all sorts of rumours as to why my great grandmother had given up her children as soon as they were born and that she hadn't given up her last daughter. My grandad would never talk about them. He would only say that he was unwanted and was "dumped" on another family who didn't really care for him, that he slept under the stairs and his parents never married.

Being a parent myself, I could not think of a single reason for giving up any one of my five children, which has often made me wonder what made my great grandparents give up theirs.

Diane has visualised one reason somebody may have gone through this, and I will be eternally grateful for her romanticism of this unusual situation.

Unfortunately, I doubt this was the story at the time.

THE BIRTHDAY PRESENT

It began with a look. Not a look of passion, nor a look of desperate longing but a look, nonetheless.

"Can I help you sir?"

"Yes, at least I hope so."

She giggled.

"So, do I sir. If not I'm in the wrong job." He managed a smile, although she was not sure if it was a smile or a sneer.

"I need a birthday present for my wife. She is with child, so nothing too fitted."

"How about a nice hat and gloves. These arrived this morning." She gestured towards a rather lovely plum coloured hat, with a wide brim and large cream feather. "We also have gloves to match and a parasol, should your wife be struggling with the summer sun."

He thought for a moment.

"Surely, one does not need a parasol and gloves?"

She rolled her eyes. Clearly, this man clearly did not understand accessorizing. She sighed, a little louder than intended.

"Excuse me," he muttered having been caught off guard.

"I bet she's one of those damn suffragettes. I can't abide free thinking women."

"They are all made of the finest silk."

"How much for the hat and gloves?" This was the first time he properly looked at her. She was pretty enough, although her dress suggested she was an assistant and not the owner.

"13 shillings sir. As I said it is the finest silk."

"And how much for the parasol as well?" She really was a pretty thing with the most beautiful blue eyes. He wasn't one for shopping least of all for clothing, which he viewed as an unnecessary frivolity.

"Madame says I can do all three for 14 shillings, which is very generous given the quality of the silk."

He wasn't sure if she believed that or if it was just standard sales pitch.

"Ok, can you wrap them for me please?"

"Of course, Sir." She smiled. He felt sure she must have smiled when he entered the shop, but he hadn't noticed.

"What a beautiful smile. She's a very pretty girl, perhaps I misjudged her. Surely anyone that pretty can't be one of those confounded suffragettes."

He regularly referred all free-thinking women as battle axes that were long past their prime, along with an opinion that free-thinking women were the curse of the 1900's. This of course did not include Queen Victoria, who in contrast was a wonderful woman and a shining example to all.

"Have you worked here long?" He asked, slightly embarrassed at his feeble attempt to make polite conversation. She was less nervous.

"Since I were a young girl, I began as a seamstress when I were only 10 or 11 years old. Some of the dresses in here I still make, but not so often. Not these days."

With a head full of the pretty shop assistant, on March the 26th 1904, he left for home.

Percy, for that was his name, delivered the package to his pregnant wife on her birthday. She, of course nodded, smiled, and made all the correct appreciative noises. She was as grateful as a woman in her uncomfortable condition could be.

"I love it Perce – thank you." She even ventured a brisk kiss on his cheek before disappearing downstairs to open the pub. He knew she wouldn't like it and that the kiss was as much of a token as his gift had been. A token was exactly how he viewed their marriage; a token gesture designed to give an air of respectability.

DAISY

Daisy was what one politely called flighty, pretty enough certainly, but she had an eye for one of the local lads; Jack Skipton. Jack was a journalist for the local evening paper. He covered crime and as such was equally disliked by both the police and the crooks they arrested. Due to the lack of any real crime on the Island he regularly satirised the former and outwardly mocked petty criminals. Of course, the public adored him and none more so than Daisy. Unfortunately for Daisy, Jack had a roving eye, and Daisy was just one of his many dalliances. It would be foolish to believe that her parents had not warned her against chasing after such men as Jack Skipton, but like all young modern women she was apt to do as she pleased. And a lot of good that did her.

It was a frosty November morning when the sun hung so low in the sky, bathing the world in the pale glow of lost summer days, that

Mr Welton stood on his doorstep taking in the crisp fresh air. His niece Daisy on the other hand was leaning against the wall smoking a cigarette when Percy Ford turned the corner on his way to work. Percy, fancying himself as a bit of a gent tipped his hat and smiled.

"Mornin'" Daisy, beautiful day, isn't it?" He blushed. He always blushed when he saw her, and it always amused her that he did so.

"It sure is Percy, it sure is," she replied nonchalantly. She was fully aware of how Percy Ford, poor fool that he was, languished after her, when she was clearly besotted by the charismatic Jack Skipton.

Did Percy really think he could compete with Jack? She wondered, but only briefly as her mother always said; "'tis foolish for women to waste their time wondering what goes through a man's mind, when they were nearly always wondering what goes through a woman's mind, and of course women already know the answer to that."

Daisy finished her cigarette giving no more thought to Percy Ford, and a whole lot more thought to Jack Skipton.

It was a good couple of months later when Daisy's uncle called Percy over as he passed the house on his way to work. He passed by every morning, but beyond hat-tipping and pleasantries he had never spoken to any of the household except Daisy. She teased him something rotten, but he loved her for it. He knew she would never be his but occasionally, just occasionally, it didn't hurt to dream.

Percy didn't know if he really loved her in the way that a man should love a woman, but he was pretty sure that Jack Skipton didn't, as he had seen him out on several occasions with a different girl each time. It was true that Daisy was Jack's more regular girl, but he could tell he didn't love her, she was just a pretty distraction for a few hours.

"Good morning - Percy, isn't it?" Daisy's Uncle Charles knew Percy by sight as he worked for his father's prestigious law stationery firm. He'd had some dealings with their company when Daisy's father died, which was when he had moved into his younger brother's home. He had done so to ensure Daisy and her mother were well taken care of, in accordance with his brothers" wishes. Although Daisy was the only child still resident at the family home, and her older siblings viewed Charles" presence there as highly dubious, if not downright suspect.

"Yes Sir, can I help? Is something wrong?"

"I'm sorry to say this Nipper but yes, something is very wrong … very wrong indeed."

"Oh dear, well, in that case I hope I can be of service." Percy concluded following Daisy's uncle into the house.

Once safely inside Mr Welton continued.

"It seems our Daisy has got herself into a bit of a predicament,"

"Oh dear" Percy mused. "That doesn't sound good at all."

"I can assure you Nipper it isn't good. In fact, it's about as far from good as it gets."

Percy felt slightly affronted at being referred to as "Nipper". Once he could consider an oversight, but twice - twice required a deep breath to centre himself before continuing.

"Well, I don't really see how I can help."

"And I'm really hoping you can... help that is." Mr Welton proceeded with the speech he had been churning over in his mind for the last few days. In fact, ever since Daisy's predicament had come to his attention.

"Well now, Nipper, don't think it has escaped my attention that you are a bit sweet on our Daisy. Would that be fair to say?"

Percy was now affronted and caught off guard. Sweet on Daisy was an understatement, it seemed an even deeper breath was needed, before he answered.

"Well, er... um, I suppose so Sir."

"Quite so Nipper." A broad smile crept across Mr Welton's face.

"Call me Charles." he said thrusting a large scotch in Percy's hand.

"It's a tad early for me Sir, I've got work at 9am and it's 8.30 now. I don't mean to rush you but..."

"Yes, yes, of course, I'll cut to the chase." Percy sighed with relief as the suspense was killing him.

"Our Daisy, well she's got herself in a bit of trouble, and that scoundrel Jack Skipton might well have a way with the ladies but he's not much cop as a man. I mean, getting our girl in trouble and then denying all knowledge of it. She's respectable is our Daisy, and quite frankly I'm worried about her good reputation, what with her in the family way and with no husband so to speak. As her uncle, I naturally, feel dutybound to help her out." He could tell by Percy's expression and his deathly white pallor that the penny had dropped. Percy opened his mouth to speak but Charles Welton hastily continued before Percy could get a word in. "And so, young man I was rather hoping that you might step up and be the honourable one in a wholly dishonourable situation. Should you agree, I would of course compensate you financially. My brother had a nest egg put aside for rainy days and this would certainly qualify as one—a rainy day that is."

"Well, er, I'm not sure what to say. I mean I do like Daisy but I'm not sure she likes me much."

"Nonsense my good man, of course she does, of course she does." Percy who was somewhat unsure of the whole situation, had noted the fact that Daisy's uncle had gone from Nipper to my good man in just a few sentences.

"I need to get to work Sir, but I could pop back later with an answer if that's alright?" Percy watched Charles Welton, studying his expression closely and weighing up whether to just make a run for it. A tiny smile gradually crept across his face and Percy let out a sigh of relief, slightly more obviously than he would've liked, which was followed by one of his renowned blushes.

"That would be acceptable, now best you get along to work, and think on it Nipper." He was back to Nipper again and Percy felt sure it meant something, but he had no idea what.

"I meant what I said about compensating you, and a thousand pounds is a more than tidy sum." Percy's mouth fell open in shock, and hastily composing himself he managed a stifled goodbye before heading off to work.

That conversation dominated Percy's thoughts all day. It was true that he was sweet on Daisy, but bringing up another man's child, well, that was a big ask.

Of course, a thousand pounds would go a long way to easing the burden of such a decision. A man can do well in this world with that sort of capital.

He would do it. What had he got to lose? He did like Daisy, and generally considered her to be far beyond his grasp. She was an angel that would vanish whenever he reached out to her. He was a simple man and felt that she may well make a good wife. He wanted to believe that once she was settled into family life, she would be less ... well, less flighty. Of course, both Daisy's mother and uncle were over the moon at his acceptance, even Daisy seemed grateful. Streatham was a small place full of small minded folk and an unmarried mother would've kept them in gossip for years.

And so, on the 29th of July 1903, Percy Ford married Daisy Welton in what was a fairly low-key event, but then the Welton's had just given all their money to Percy.

The wedding took place in Ventnor on the Isle of Wight. Percy had spent some time there with his parents and had always felt he may live there some day. It was certainly a good place to start married life. Percy felt content. He had married the girl of his dreams and been paid for the pleasure. The only thing Percy didn't get was his nuptials, and being somewhat less experienced than his wife, he believed her that it wasn't right to do such things in pregnancy. It was going to be a long time before he could fully experience his new bride, and he could only hope her experience would be of benefit to him when the time finally came.

Charles Welton of course made his feelings on their marriage perfectly clear, practically hi-jacking Percy as he headed for the gents.

"Now just you make sure you take care of our Daisy. Remember you're not too big for me to batty fang if you upset her." These words echoed round Percy's head as he watched him leave. Charles Welton had a way about him that couldn't help but unnerve Percy, but then, that was the intention.

They had been married a little over a week when Daisy came downstairs looking quite distraught for someone recently married. More than anything he hoped her uncle didn't see her looking that miserable. Charles Welton was a formidable man on a good day and not somebody Percy wished to cross.

Daisy's day had started very badly, having got out of bed, and attended to her toilet needs she had discovered her monthly period had started. She slumped down on the toilet unsure what her next move should be. She was married to a good man, there was no denying that. Percy Ford had literally made an honest woman of her, but she didn't love him and certainly didn't find him attractive. Not like her Jack as she viewed him, except Jack wasn't hers, Percy was.

She had to do something. It was all such a mess. On the one hand her uncle would have her guts for garters if he found out she didn't need to be married, especially given how much it had cost him to find her a husband. On the other hand, not being pregnant gave her no real excuse for not being a "proper wife" to her new husband. She needed to get pregnant and quickly. There was nothing else for it, she would visit Jack Skipton and arrange a liaison with him sooner rather than later. In the meanwhile, she needed to hide her current state from everyone – especially Percy.

It was two weeks later when Daisy had her clandestine meeting with Jack Skipton. Daisy had gone to London to visit her mother and while there took full advantage of the situation.

Jack had never turned a pretty girl away in his adult life and Daisy just wanted to be pregnant. It would be longer than Daisy anticipated, and several more visits to her mother before she finally achieved her goal.

Charles Welton eyed Daisy with suspicion. Daisy in response shifted uncomfortably in her chair. Daisy and Percy had married in July and to all intents and purposes she should have been much further on in her pregnancy than she appeared. Percy was suspicious, as was her uncle. However, her uncle was much more vocal than her husband with his opinion.

Charles had been in Ventnor conducting some business as he put it and had decided to take the still newlyweds Percy and Daisy out for lunch.

"You're not as large as your mother was with you."

It was an announcement not a question which Daisy deflected with a gaze that would turn the milk sour. She no more liked her uncle than she did Ventnor. Both, she viewed as dangerously insipid. She missed London, her mother and of course Jack.

"And pray tell me Uncle," she spat venomously. "What would any man know about bringing children into the world, apart from the bit that suits them well enough."

"Daisy Welton, I mean Ford - sorry Percy -that is no way for a lady to speak. If you weren't a married woman, I'd clip yer one. Lord, love us, it's a good job yer mother's not here."

"Well, I'll thank you Uncle, not to be questioning me on matters that don't concern you."

With that Charles sat in silence although his stern expression remained. Percy felt it was best to abstain from mentioning

17

the whole thing, as his own father would often say, 'it is better to be silent and thought a mouse than to be considered a foolish lion.' More than anything he was grateful that Daisy hadn't tried to involve him in the whole sorry discussion.

Daisy however, seized this as an opportunity to leave, dragging Percy with her.

"He's got a point." Percy ventured as Daisy slammed the restaurant door behind her.

"Oh, not you too ... saints preserve us. You're an expert on childbirth too are you, Percy Ford?"

Percy hung his head. There was nothing to be gained by arguing with her. Instead, they walked home in silence.

"Daisy really? Again? You're gonna get caught by that husband of yours if you're not careful."

"Percy?" She laughed. "He's an oblivious fool on a good day – and even if he did notice, he wouldn't say anything. He's too scared of my uncle and anyway, he's besotted by me."

"Well, that maybe, but you know a man only has so much energy. You are voracious that's fer sure. I need a bit of time off too."

"I won't come tomorrow, I promise. "

"I was thinking of a more permanent break. I've met this girl y'see?"

Daisy saw perfectly.

Daisy was mortified but she knew he was right, and somewhere deep in the back of her mind she had always known Jack would never be hers. She had only ever been a bit of fun.

"We had fun though, didn't we?" He offered.

Daisy nodded, tears prickling her eyes.

Despite the heartbreak, she reminded herself of how much she had risked, sneaking out of her mother's house late at night to visit Jack with one sole purpose—to get pregnant.

"One last... for old time's sake?" She nudged him. When all

was said and done, he was a man, and she was a pretty girl. So, he nodded, pulled her close, kissed her and slowly unbuttoned her dress for the last time.

It was only a few weeks. In fact, it was around about the same time the banns were read in church announcing the intended marriage of Jack Skipton and Laura Marsh, that Daisy first skipped her monthly time.

She was sad that Jack had found someone other than her, but she would always have his child, that was something. She knew Percy and her uncle weren't fools they would work it out soon enough. However, it would keep Percy away from her, for a bit longer.

Percy wasn't an ugly or hideous man. Truth to tell he was clean, smart, and hardworking and most women would have considered him a catch. Just not Daisy.

A CHANCE ENCOUNTER

"Good morning, Sir?"

Percy blushed. It was the pretty shop assistant, who had sold him his wife's birthday present.

"Did your wife like the gloves?" She smiled. He blushed.

"Er, yes she did thank you." He eventually managed.

He remembered her pretty eyes and soft voice and had thought of her often. Before her, there had only ever been Daisy. He had loved Daisy from the day he set eyes on her, but now, things were different. Daisy was not how he had imagined her. She was never going to love him, that much was evident, and he knew the child she carried had been conceived after their marriage. He also knew that the baby growing in his wife's belly was probably Jack Skipton's. More importantly, he was fast falling out of love with her, especially now he had come across someone who seemed genuinely pleased to see him.

"I love this place it's so, well, so tranquil. Don't you think?"

"Yes, I suppose it is." He smiled back at her and gestured for her to join him. It was his favourite park where he could watch the world go by. It was somewhere that seemed beyond time, a place where children played, dogs were walked, and lovers met in secret.

She smiled, but politely declined.

"I have to be at work in ten minutes, but hopefully our paths will cross again very soon."

Percy smiled back at her. Not only would their paths cross again, but they would cross daily, and for the next few years.

Percy knew that day that he was besotted by her. She was everything his wife was not, but he was married to Daisy, and he had married her for better or worse, and she was pregnant. It may not have been his child, but he had made a promise to her and her uncle; a promise to look after her and her baby and a gentleman keeps his promise.

JACK ARRIVES

"Come quick, come quick. Fetch Lucy Jones, the baby's coming. Hurry Percy! Hurry!"

Percy dropped his hat 3 times on his way out the door and tutted himself every time.

"Hurry Percy, hurry. For the love of God, just go!"

He raced down the street to Lucy's house. Lucy was one of the newly trained midwives. Most local women made do with Mother Bennet as she was known, an old woman who had delivered many a nipper. However, Percy knew Daisy's mother and uncle would never forgive him, if she didn't get the best care possible. Of course, new, properly trained midwives weren't cheap, but then, neither was Daisy.

Percy may have been a gentleman, but he was also a man. The arrival of Daisy's mother, who scolded him for being in the way, as he opened the door to her seemed a good opportunity to escape. Three women, engaged in the art of childbirth was far more chaos and yoppul than any man needed.

"Going for a walk in the park." He shouted as he put his hat on. There was a general mumbling of acknowledgement, and he headed off to enjoy the day. He didn't want Daisy to suffer, but, when all was said and done, it wasn't his child. Percy no more wanted someone else's bastard, than Daisy wanted Percy.

The sun was shining, and the sky was blue, and despite his wife's screams, which grew fainter with each step, the day was almost perfect. Perfection of course, could be achieved by reaching the park early enough to encounter the pretty shop assistant, whose face filled his waking hours.

She was there, sat on a bench reading the morning paper. Percy wasn't sure what to make of it. He had never met a woman who actually read the papers before. Daisy pretended to, but it was half hearted; reading the newspapers was still the domain of men.

Prior to this moment he had only ever known women to read books, and usually ones written by other women. Nonetheless, there she was as pretty as any woman could be, and yet as bold as brass sat on a bench reading a newspaper. She must have been able to sense him there as she lowered her paper, looked up at him, and smiled. It was the most perfect smile Percy had ever seen. His heart melted. She could read as many papers as she liked, as long as she smiled at him.

"Would you care to join me?" She patted the seat beside her. She was as bold as she was beautiful, and he was unable to resist her.

"Thank you," he manged as he tentatively sat down next to her.

"What are you reading?" He asked, smiling back at her. He didn't care what, he just wanted her to sit beside him forever.

"Can you keep a secret?" He nodded, his head firmly in the clouds.

"I'm just keeping up to date with the suffragette movement. Every day is one day nearer to women getting the vote. It's too exciting..." her voice tailed off and she smiled, her eyes shining in the summer sunlight. "...You do believe women should have the vote, don't you?"

"Oh yes." He ventured back. "Of course, I do."

He didn't especially object to women having the vote, more that he found the militant activities of the suffragettes most disagreeable behaviour for the fairer sex, and that the women engaged in such activities were equally unattractive.

"Good." She beamed, "as I have to confess to being an avid supporter. I've been following the movement as long as I can remember and feel very much a part of it. Don't get me wrong I'm no Emmeline Pankhurst—wish I was, but I attended one of her meetings back last year at her home in Manchester. So, I feel akin to them, and I do believe I would do almost anything they asked of me. I'm so glad you approve of our cause. I believe we shall get along fine."

Percy was completely thrown off guard, he found it hard to imagine a girl with such a lovely smile could have anything to do with such undignified behaviour. He felt his mind wandering back to her soft voice and pretty face.

"Actually," she interrupted his wandering thoughts. "it's my day off. Shall we get some lunch, or do you have to be somewhere? Oh, I almost forgot, I'm Elsie—Elsie Simmonds."

His mind flashed back at once to the screaming Daisy, his moaning mother-in-law, the midwife that had so far cost him an arm and a leg ... and of course the bastard offspring.

"I'm Percy—Percy Ford and I'd love to—have lunch that is." He smiled somewhat awkwardly.

Before Elsie he hadn't considered that there could be another woman for him beyond Daisy. Yet here he was, abandoning his wife to have lunch with a woman he knew very little about, but wanted to know everything about.

She linked her arm in his, and so it began.

It would be somewhere around dessert that his father's apprentice tracked him down and called him to one side.

"Mrs Ford's had the baby Sir, her mother thought you should know. It's a boy Sir, you must be right proud?"

"Indeed, I am lad, and thank you for finding me. Here's a shillin' and don't tell my father otherwise he'll think he pays me too much."

"I won't Sir." And with that the lad raced off back to work.

Percy made his apologies to Elsie and said he would buy her lunch the following week to make up for cutting it short this time.

"I'll hold you to that Percy Ford." Elsie laughed. He smiled back lost in her eyes that twinkled and danced.

"It's a date." He finally managed with a smile before heading home to meet Daisy's child.

"Jack Clarence Roadway Ford" Daisy announced.

"That's a lot of name for such a tiny boy. Still, I don't suppose I need to wonder who his father is ..."

Daisy scowled.

"Clarence after me, Roadway after your mother, and ...

"... and will Jack Skipton be paying for his son?" Percy continued undaunted by Daisy's angry expression.

"I'm sure I don't know what you mean Percy Ford. Isn't he your son?"

"Look Daisy, I know I agreed to bring him up as such, but don't insult my intelligence. You, and I both know he's not mine and truth to tell, I also know his father is Jack Skipton and don't try to pretend otherwise."

Daisy had not long brought her son into the world, and wasn't at her best to say the least, so was very unwilling to get into an argument with Percy over paternity. The thought, however, did flash through her mind that this may give her leverage to end this farce of a marriage before it started.

"I need to rest. I am exhausted and ask that should you insist, we discuss this matter later."

Percy was at a loss. He hadn't meant to be so hard on Daisy, after all she had been, and still was someone he cared very much about. He had hoped she might learn to love him once they were married. She did not. He had had also hoped that once the baby was here, that perhaps she might become more of a wife. That too, was looking unlikely, but then, he had intended to be a good, loving, and loyal husband, yet at this precise moment in time he was none of those things. So, he left the room, leaving Daisy to do battle with her demons, while he wrestled with his own.

Percy and Daisy's relationship was never conventional. Their marriage had never been consummated, at least not with each other. Daisy had bestowed all her affections on Jack Skipton and when that finished, she devoted all her attention solely towards his son. Percy had consummated his marriage mostly alone, until eventually he had sought solace with one of the Island's many ladies of the night; those always willing to offer comfort to a man less loved. It had proven expensive and not what he really wanted. Elsie, that's what, or rather who he really wanted. Elsie with her pretty smile, twinkly eyes, and lust for life. Elsie wasn't Daisy. Daisy had a lust alright but not for life, and definitely not for Percy.

LOTS TO SMILE ABOUT

Percy smiled at the sunlight peeking through the gap in the curtains and turned to face Elsie.

"What're you smiling at? Eh, Percy Ford?"

"Lots – I have lots to smile about today. But I'd better be going soon, or she'll be after me."

"I wish you didn't have to go. In fact, I wish you never had to go." Elsie giggled and squeezed him tighter. Percy laughed—it was hard not to. He had never been this happy and he too wished he didn't have to go, but he did.

"Will I see you tomorrow?"

"You always ask me that and the answer is always yes, you know that. I can't not see you—not ever!"

"Good." Elsie purred stretching lazily, revealing just enough to remind Percy what he was missing out on by leaving.

"I'm sure my soul would die without you," she half whispered with breathless seduction, "truly it would."

32

He could see her reflection in the mirror as he straightened his tie. There was no denying her beauty and despite all his previous thoughts concerning modern women, there was something about Elsie that made his heart beat faster, and his world a lot brighter.

He kissed her gently and headed for the door, reaching it just in time to hear Elsie's parting words. The same breathless panting and the same words she always used.

"Goodbye my love. Hurry back as my soul is fading fast."

Percy held his head high, and practically skipped home, as he had done ever since their secret romance began. He had made love to the beautiful Elsie many times and he loved her more with every step, every breath, and every beat of his heart. She consumed him, she had devoured his soul and now she owned him. There was quite simply no room left in his heart for Daisy or her son Jack.

He knew he had to end it and be completely with Elsie. He

would've married her the next day, if not sooner, had he been free to do so. But he wasn't, and that needed rectifying.

Percy rubbed his eyes and smiled as the sun peeked in through the heavy drapes.

He felt sure that it was going to be a good day. It was a day to address matters that he had left unaddressed for far too long.

He had done well for himself, having used the thousand pounds that Daisy's Uncle Charles had given him wisely. He had invested the money in the old saltwater bath house on Ventnor Esplanade, refurbished it and business was flourishing. So, now was as good a time as any to talk to Daisy about their future.

He had a well-prepared speech, that he had rehearsed in his head over, and over, and over again. So, once he was settled at the breakfast table he began.

"Daisy, I'd like to talk about our future."

Daisy wanted to point out that they didn't have a past let alone a future, but politely bit her lip.

"I know that you have no affection for me, and that is fine ..."

"Oh, Percy, you're not going to pretend you care for me or Jack, are you? Because I am fully aware you only married me because my uncle bullied and bribed you to into doing so."

Percy slowly shook his head.

"I married you because I liked you very much. I thought I loved you, having been smitten by you since you came into my father's shop with your uncle. From the moment I saw you I was quite captivated, but I was under no illusions. I knew you were besotted by Jack Skipton. However, I had hoped once we were married you would learn to love me. I also know now that is something that will never happen. Likewise, I know, as I'm sure does everyone else, that Jack was conceived after our wedding, No doubt during one of your many trips to the mainland."

Daisy hung her head, the truth was painful, but it was the truth.

"What're you saying Percy. Am I to be thrown out onto the street, with a babe in arms?"

"Good Lord Daisy! I'm saying no such thing. Look here, I have met someone, and I'm pretty sure you have too. I've seen you mooning after Stan Pearson ..."

"He's married and well you know it." Daisy rapidly interjected and leapt up ready to storm off. But not before adding "Just because you have a fancy woman, it doesn't mean the rest of us do."

"Oh, Daisy for the love of God stop. I'm not stupid and I have eyes. I'm simply trying to make a proposal that will suit us all. One I think you will agree to."

Daisy sat back down but remained poised, ready to storm out should his proposal offend her.

"This is a large building, and despite the fact that we don't love each other, I do care for you Daisy.

Very much so, and although I am not his father, I find myself protective of your son. Perhaps not as much as a father would be, but I certainly wouldn't see the lad out on the street. I'm not a monster. I am simply proposing that as this is a large building, we move our bed chambers further apart. Much further apart. I will move Elsie in, and she can be, in name only, our housekeeper. And you will be free to entertain whoever you please. I think that as long as we are discreet, this could work. You would still be the lady of the house and your boy would continue to have a roof over his head."

"And what of your Elsie?" Daisy enquired, "is she happy with this?"

"I believe she will be. Right now, I am more interested in your thoughts."

Daisy nodded.

Despite her protests she and Stan Pearson were well and truly in love with each other. His wife was ill and not expected to last too much longer, at which point they intended to marry.

Percy had heard rumours to this effect and was quite happy to provide Daisy with a roof over her head until such time arose.

"So, what do you think?" Percy beamed at Elsie, having explained his plan post coitus.

"I love it, almost as much as I love you. I love the subterfuge. I shall be your covert mistress. Oh, the drama Percy, it is sublime, almost beyond words. And truthfully, I will make you sing, dance, and dream." Elsie snuggled up to him, she fitted so well in his arms, something she had pointed out during their first lover's tryst.

"You know I don't actually mind being your housekeeper, all great love stories should have the Master of the house falling in love with his housekeeper."

Percy pulled her closer.

"I love you." He whispered softly.

MOVING IN

"So, you're the new housekeeper?" Daisy announced from the doorway, deliberately loud enough for any passers-by to hear.

Elsie smiled. She knew exactly what Daisy was doing.

"Yes Ma'am." She nodded and curtseyed, equally loud enough for people to hear. "And I hope you're not intimidated by a younger woman in your home." She whispered the second sentence just loud enough for Daisy to hear.

Daisy's cheeks flushed a glorious shade of scarlet. Elsie winked at her, and Daisy decided enough was enough. She closed the front door on the street and glared at Elsie.

Unfortunately for Daisy, Elsie was oblivious to this.

"Right, young lady," she announced loudly enough to get Elsie's attention. "Let's get something straight. You are my husband's doxy and nothing more and I am not required to do anything more than tolerate your presence here. Are we clear?" As much as Elsie wanted to call Daisy a frigid old woman, she decided this would not do her any favours.

"Abundantly clear... *Ma'am.*"

Daisy was irritated by the sarcastic tone in Elsie's voice. Both women eyed each other from across the room, and it was hard to tell which one cast the eviler eye. Either would have given Medusa a run for her money. The glaring exchange between the two women was brought to an abrupt end by Percy returning home.

"Ah, you've met then. Is everything alright?"

Both women nodded and smiled.

"You know, I have a really good feeling about this. Come on Else, I'll show you to your room, and then we'll have some supper."

Percy opened the door for Elsie who glanced over her shoulder at Daisy. Daisy stuck her tongue out in defiance at Elsie. She may have won the battle, but as far as Daisy

was concerned the war had only just
begun.

BRAZEN

Daisy peered up from her morning paper. It wasn't any of the same ones that Elsie would read. A local rag nothing more. She watched Elsie pouring the tea for Percy who was still as gooey eyed over her as he had been when he had first met her.

Daisy was unnerved by Elsie, after all, they were both modern women. Daisy had an eye for the men, something no respectable wife and mother should have. Whereas Elsie loved one man, wholeheartedly and absolutely. Daisy admired her for that, but Elsie had a different sort of wildness about her. She was brazen in her beliefs, especially her belief that women should have the same rights as men, specifically the right to vote. She made no bones about her beliefs either.

Daisy had her own concerns where Elsie was concerned, especially this particular morning. She waited until Percy and Jack had left the room—she had practically shooed them out.

"Elsie, could I have a word please?"

"Why certainly Ma'am."

"Don't do that Elsie, we both know you are more than a housekeeper, so don't pretend otherwise. I'm no more your mistress than you are mine. Don't get me wrong I like our little arrangement as much as you and Percy, but I am worried things may change."

Elsie sighed,"

"I'm not keeping it" she ventured. "If that's your concern?"

"It was one of my concerns, yes. Does Percy know?"

"No, he doesn't suspect anything, and like I said we don't want children, well not yet, not until after we get the vote. Daisy rolled her eyes, but Elsie continued regardless. When I go to the meetings in London, some of us are very proactive. Yes, proactive that's the right word. It can get quite dangerous, it's no place for a babe."

"Well, in that case you'll need to go away. I have friends in Brighton you can go there for your confinement. When you return, I will arrange for some friends to meet you. They are desperate for a baby and will happily take it off you. I reckon they'd pay you for it, too."

"And what about Percy? He has every right to have a say in this."

"No, he doesn't he is a man and therefore knows nothing of babies."

Elsie's eyes narrowed. Daisy was infuriating at the best of times.

"I'll think about it."

And with that Elsie went about her day.

It was hard for her to concentrate on anything beyond her current predicament. On the one hand Daisy made a fair argument, after all she could easily spend a few months on the mainland on the pretext of a suffragette campaign. But, on the other hand it was the love of her life's child and surely he should have a say in the matter. Deep within her heart she knew she would have to say something to Percy. They had sworn never to have secrets from each other. Equally, they had decided not to have children until such time as women had the vote, and Elsie was free to concentrate on being a mother.

They both wanted children, just not yet.

The conversation, however, did not take place until much later, as Elsie undressed for bed. Percy lay back watching her comb through her long dark hair. He thought how beautiful she looked and felt certain nothing could ever change that.

"Percy," she began tentatively. "I have something to discuss with you, something important." He noted the gravity in her tone and sought hard for the right words to reassure her, but none came.

"What is it, Elsie? What's wrong?" Was the best he could manage.

"I am with child, and Daisy said -"

"Wait, what's Daisy got to do with it?"

"Daisy could tell that I was carrying a child and suggested -"

"And exactly what did Daisy suggest?" The words came out a far more sternly than he had intended, being somewhat irritated at his wife's involvement.

"Please Percy," Elsie implored and Percy realising her distress hung his head, softened his tone of voice, and begged her to continue.

"Daisy suggested," she paused waiting for the next interruption but there was none.

"Daisy suggested that I go to England and have the baby. She knows a couple who are desperate for a child and would be happy to adopt. They'd pay us too."

"So, Daisy has it all worked out, does she?" said Percy bitterly, once again, instantly regretting it.

Elsie sat on the bed and began to cry.

"I'm sorry Else, I didn't mean to upset you and I'm sure Daisy was just trying to help. I'm just not sure who she was trying to help."

Percy held Elsie tightly. He could feel her heartbeat and he stroked her hair trying to make up for his earlier severity. In those silent moments he considered the situation with more clarity.

They had agreed children were off the table until Elsie was free to devote her time to motherhood. Although Percy had grown up with a dislike of suffragettes, he very much admired this one. Any opinion he had of them was instilled in him by his father, who he now realised knew nothing of suffragettes—or love.

He wished for a world where he and Elsie were free to love each other, have children, and for her to be allowed to continue her work in the Women's Movement. He pondered the idea that perhaps, this was the world Elsie was fighting for; one where their daughters would have the same freedom as their son's. Perhaps, just perhaps, this world would be a better one.

"You know, I will support your decision. I love you and whatever is right for you is right for me. We had agreed on no children, so getting the baby adopted is preferable to any other backstreet or quack methods." Elsie shuddered at the thought of a back street abortion, and clung tighter to Percy.

"I hadn't considered anything else, not even a hot bath and gin."

"It's alright my love, as soon as you need to, you can leave for the mainland, and I will follow a few days later. I know the couple Daisy is referring to, and they are good people and will be good parents. It matters not that they pay for the child, but I will ensure that you are well cared for, and your expenses reimbursed. At such time as the child is born, he or she will need to be registered, all I ask is that you name me as their father. A child, adopted or otherwise should know it's origins."

Elsie hugged Percy tighter still before kissing him in that way that all men long to be kissed.

THE JOURNEY HOME

It was a chilly, late October Morning when Percy, Elsie, and their baby daughter boarded the ferry to return to the island.

The journey home was difficult, and Percy could see this wasn't an easy decision for Elsie. She was unusually quiet for one so full of life, and the journey couldn't end soon enough. The weather was as miserable as they were. And it had started to rain by the time Elsie, Percy, and a baby girl with no name reached the registry office in Newport. They were greeted by the couple Daisy had made all the adoption arrangements with a Robert and Doris Miller.

Elsie smiled weakly as she hesitantly handed the precious bundle over to Doris.

"Did you give her a name?" The woman smiled at Elsie.

"No," replied Percy. "We thought that should be your job, but please list her us as her parents on the birth certificate. I hate the thought of her not knowing where she came from."

"Of course, old man. Of course." Robert said patting him reassuringly on the back.

"Have you got a name in mind?" Elsie quietly questioned.

"We have a couple of thoughts. Would you like to hear them?"

"No thank you Doris, I think we're better off not knowing, don't you Percy?"

Percy nodded.

"I think we'd best be getting home now."

"Of course, of course old man. I almost forgot."

Robert handed Percy a thick envelope.

"But, but... we didn't... I mean we hadn't ..."

"Nonsense. Nonsense, old man. Take it, she's worth every penny to us. Buy the wife something nice."

Wife. Neither Percy nor Elsie had ever heard her referred to as his wife, but neither of them corrected him.

"Thank you." Percy whispered. "Kiss her goodbye from us, won't you please?"

They nodded and headed into the registry office.

Percy and Elsie headed home in silence.

ELSIE'S CONDITION

Elsie returned home from a suffragette rally, and immediately took to her bed, claiming she felt nauseous.

"Percy, be a darling and fetch me some warm milk, that should settle it."

It didn't and for the next few days she continued to ail.

On the fourth day over dinner Percy suggested to Daisy that he might fetch the doctor.

"Really Percy. Just how naive are you? She's pregnant again you damn fool!"

Percy looked at Daisy, his mouth had dropped open, and the colour was rapidly draining from his face.

"Percy, Percy... Oh, for the love of God Percy snap out of it and pay attention..."

"...But we've been really careful since. Well, you know?"

"Clearly not careful enough. So have you got any ideas?" Percy continued to stare at her dumbstruck.

"I thought not," continued Daisy. "Well, maybe, and it is only a maybe. There's a young couple who come in the baths that are struggling to conceive. I could have a word if you like? You'd better talk to Elsie first. And for God's sake Percy, learn to keep it in your trousers."

"It's not just me you know?" he mumbled, taking his leave.

"Elsie." He whispered nudging her gently.

She yawned and stretched, and he thought how beautiful she was. There was a rosy glow about her. Of course, it may just have been the sunset streaming in through the window, but either way she looked lovely.

"Elsie, I have something to ask you."

She smiled.

"I take it you've spoken to Daisy then?"

He nodded.

"She doesn't miss a trick, does she? Well, once again she's right. I'm pregnant. I don't suppose she knows any more childless couples, does she?"

Percy wasn't sure what to say. He hadn't expected her to be so open.

"As a matter of fact, she said she might know a couple."

"I see. Well, it's your child too—what do you think?"

"Honestly Elsie, I'm not sure what to think. I mean we said no children, until you are free from the movement."

"I know, and I love you for it, but how many children do we get adopted, before you hate me ... and the suffragette movement?"

"Oh, I could never hate you. You're far too precious to me. Surely, you know that. And I would have a thousand children adopted before I lost you."

The tears welled up in Elsie's eyes and she almost threw herself into his arms.

"I love you, Percy Ford."

Percy smiled and held her so tight; she almost couldn't breathe.

"I'll let you sleep and tell Daisy to sound out this couple she knows.

Once again Percy and Elsie made the journey to the mainland for her confinement. Percy had bought a holiday cottage for him and Elsie, which was proving to be a convenient location to spend her pregnancy. It was in the West Country and far enough from the towns to avoid attracting any unwanted attention. It was near a little cove and Elsie loved it there.

MARGIE KING

The journey back home with the baby was difficult. Elsie was obviously distressed at having to give up another baby, and Percy never let go of her hand. On top of this the wind was strong, and the crossing rough. Percy felt seasick but he was determined not to let it show. Elsie needed him and that was more important.

They stepped off the ferry and made their way to Newport, where this time they were greeted by Daisy's best friend, Margie King.

"I'll take him from here. Daisy thought it might be best."

"Did Daisy now?" Percy scowled. "Well, it's not best. I'd like to meet the parents of our child. I'm guessing they're nearby. So, I'd thank you to fetch them. Now please!"

Margie scuttled of to fetch the new parents.

Percy saw a tear roll down Elsie's face as she held her baby tighter.

"She didn't even ask if the babe was a boy or a girl. Are you sure we are doing the right thing Percy?"

"I hope so, but we'll have a better idea when the couple get here." He gently squeezed her hand, before adding "and I'll be having words with Daisy, when we get back."

Elsie managed a weak smile, and moments later Margie reappeared with the couple. They weren't as young as the couple who had adopted their first child. They must have been in their early thirties, but the woman had a kind face, and they looked well turned out.

"Boy or girl?" The man almost whispered.

"Boy." Percy replied. "If you would indulge me, I have but one request to make of you. That is, that my name be on the birth certificate. I think it is important for children to know their origins."

"Couldn't agree more Sir. I was adopted myself. Consider it done, What's your name?"

"Percy—Percy Ford"

"Well, shall we name him Percy? Percy Reginald Ford shall be his birth name. I'm Reginald by the way, and this is my wife, Georgia."

Georgia leant forward and touched Elsie's arm gently.

"We'll register the baby as having been born in Brading, where we live. Would that be alright?"

Elsie managed a weak smile and nodded; her eyes were beginning to water again.

"Thank you," Percy smiled. And with that Percy and Elsie made the journey home in silence.

ELSIE AND DAISY

"Elsie Simmonds – you just hang on a moment." Elsie stopped still. She could tell by the tone in Daisy's voice that she knew. She always knew before Percy. There'd been occasions when Daisy had known before she did.

"You have got to be joking – what's wrong with you? Can't you leave him be for 5 minutes?"

"I don't really see how that's anything to do with you Daisy. It's not as if you want him now, is it?"

"No Elsie, I don't, but given the amount of babies you're pushing out, I doubt he'll want you much longer."

Elsie scowled. She could feel the tears beginning to form and fought hard to hold them back. There was no way she was giving Daisy the satisfaction of knowing she'd hurt her.

"You don't see me getting pregnant, do you?"

"Aren't you a little old?" Elsie smiled back at her, delighted to be giving Daisy a taste of her own bitter medicine.

Daisy was angry but did not want to lose face, so, taking a deep breath she calmly replied.

"Why no Elsie, I'm just reaching my prime if you must know. Oh, and while I think of it get yourself a sponge."

Elsie stuck her nose in the air and left.

Of course, none of this altered the fact that Elsie was pregnant, and that she would need to find someone to bring this one up.

The sun streamed in through the window, and she stared out at the world below. She watched mothers and governesses pushing perambulators, and wondered if she was missing out. Should she give up the cause and settle into motherhood?

She kicked off her shoes and lay back on the bed. Of course, it wasn't just the cause, there was Percy to consider, and Jack. He may not be Percy's son, and they may have had a difficult start, but these days Percy loved him as his own. Her having a child would complicate everything, and as much as Daisy infuriated her, she had no wish to humiliate her, well, maybe, but only for a moment or two.

Basking in the autumn sunlight, and lost in her thoughts, she had become oblivious to the time. It wasn't until she heard Percy coming up the stairs that she realised how late it was.

She leapt up and practically flung herself into his arms.

"I s'pose Daisy's already told you." She whispered relaxing her grip on him.

He nodded.

"She said you two had words, and you said some very cruel things to her—did you?"

"I told her I was surprised she needed to bother with birth control methods at her age. It wasn't my proudest moment." She looked down at the floor, sheepishly.

"It damn well shoulda been." Percy laughed "She needs putting in her place. I'm so proud of you." Elsie too began to giggle.

"She was kinda asking for it, but she may have a point. I'm not sure how many more times I can do this."

"We agreed, and I'm more willing to give up a hundred babies before I see you forced into motherhood before you're ready. I tell you what let's go out for dinner and I'll contact Reginald and Georgia tomorrow. They said to get in touch if we had any more mishaps."

"They did say that, didn't they? I swear Percy Ford you are a genius, and I couldn't love you more if I tried."

Reginald and Georgia were delighted to have another baby boy to look after, and as before they included the name Ford. Alfred George Ford, after Reginald's father, Georgia, and of course, Percy Ford. This time Elsie had gone to stay with them for several months and left a week after Alfred was born.

It was a glorious Summer "s day when Percy went to fetch her. The sun was shining, the flowers were in bloom, the whole world seemed vibrant, and beautiful. The whole world, except Percy.

"That was the worst, he said glumly. I don't care if we have to do this again, but I am not letting you out of my sight for that long ever again. Not ever Elsie Simmonds—you hear me?"

Elsie nodded and smiled weakly. She was tired, it had been a long labour and she too had felt the pain of separation, having spent so long away from Percy. When they returned to Ventor, Elsie was exhausted, and Percy could see this. He swore he would never let her go through anything alone again.

"I love you Else – more than life itself. "He whispered tucking her into bed.

A SURPRISE BOOKING

Over the last few weeks breakfast had become a fractious experience in the Ford, Welton, and Ellis household. Daisy would peer at Elsie suspiciously looking for signs of another pregnancy. Elsie would scowl back at her, irritated by the implication. She was still bleeding from the last baby, which had come three weeks earlier than intended.

Percy and Jack would generally eat in silence, rolling their eyes periodically, at either each other or the women. By early March Percy had, had enough.

"I've booked a cabin for myself and Elsie on a ship to America—we leave on Friday."

"But that's only 3 days away." Daisy gasped.

Elsie looked just as surprised as Daisy.

"I'm sorry, but it was going to be a surprise." He beamed at Elsie.

"It is! I need to pack. You haven't given me much time," Elsie stood up to leave, and then plonked herself back down.

"What about the movement? There are things planned for the summer. How long are we going for? When will we be back?" She got up again, leaned across the breakfast table, almost knocking Daisy's plate off. Fortunately, Daisy grabbed it in time, and while Daisy juggled the plate and its contents Elsie proceeded to kiss Percy firmly on the lips.

"Really Elsie, there's a child present. But, it's a fair question. Exactly when are you intending to return?" Daisy practically squawked at them. Jack, on the other hand was just grateful for the lack of tension.

"When we get back!" Elsie announced defiantly. "Anyway, why do you want to know? Will you miss me? Or do you have plans of your own?" Elsie raised an eyebrow at Daisy.

"My plans are no concern of yours, Elsie Simmonds. What I do in my home is my affair."

"Affair being the appropriate word."

Daisy, for once was lost for words.

Elsie felt pretty smug, winked at Percy, made her apologies, such as they were and rushed off to pack.

"Well, that's that settled then." Said Percy getting up to follow Elsie and leaving a very disgruntled Daisy still clutching her breakfast plate.

"Well, I hope the weather is better in America than here," mused Elsie, watching the rain as it dripped from the guttering onto the window ledge.

"We best be getting a move on love. We sail at noon."

"Just coming." Elsie took one last look in the mirror, straightened her hat and closed the door.

Outside a car was waiting to take them to the ferry, and from there, they were to set sail from Southampton, bound for New York.

By the time they reached Southampton there was a crowd of

people gathered, all of which were jostling in an attempt to board. Percy was relieved he had spent the extra on a cabin. He and Elsie were among the first on board, and they watched as the last of the steerage hopefuls were turned away.

"It's horrible... all those people crammed downstairs. We are the lucky ones... You wait Percy Ford, when us women get the vote Things'll change. I bet one day there will be a woman Prime Minister too."

Percy nodded in the right places, and for the most part he agreed with her, but a woman Prime Minister was a stretch too far.

"Oh, Elsie," he laughed "I can't see that one happening, but I admire your optimism."

She laughed and nudged him hard in the ribs.

"You wait Percy Ford—just you wait and see. Then we'll see whose laughing." She grinned.

"Just you wait and see."

He smiled back at her. This was perfect, no Daisy peering at them disapprovingly, and he hoped Jack's life might be a bit more relaxed with him and Elsie out of the way. He was a good father to Jack and only ever wanted what was best for him, and the stress of the last month or so hadn't been good for anyone.

"Penny for them?"

"Oh, I was just thinking how much I love you, Elsie Simmonds." With that they took a last look at Southampton.

"I can see it!" Squealed an excited boy. "... I can see the Ambrose ... it's the Ambrose Lightship ... come see ... We're almost there."

Word spreads fast on a ship and Elsie and Percy joined the throng of excited passengers already gathered on deck.

"Ooh look Percy we are nearly there. This is an adventure. I can't wait to get ashore."

Percy, who had suffered some degree of sea sickness for most of the time they'd been at sea, nodded, still pale from the last bout of nausea.

"I have to admit. It'll be good to be back on dry land."

"Oh Percy, come on it'll be exciting."

Percy just nodded. He wanted to share her enthusiasm but was still feeling a little off colour.

As dry land approached Elsie squeezed Percy a little too tight. He quickly made his excuses and rushed off to find somewhere out of the way to throw up. He didn't want Elsie to see him as weak or fragile. And definitely not like this.

In a few hours their feet would be safely back on dry land and his enthusiasm would return but for now, he just needed some solitude.

AMERICA

America was wonderful, from the first look at the New York skyline it was all they had hoped for, and possibly more besides. The buildings were imposing, the people welcoming, and the lifestyle like nothing they'd ever known.

Elsie adored New York life, but Percy found it too chaotic. It was a far cry from the quiet Island life they were used to.

Elsie was in her element amid the glamorous apparel shops.

"Oh, look Percy! Those dresses, they're simply exquisite."

Elsie had an eye for beauty, especially when it came to clothes. Fortunately, she was a fair seamstress, which she attributed to a lifetime of Champagne taste, on lemonade money.

"They are no more beautiful than you could make. You know, I reckon with the right materials you could outshine all of them."

She kissed him on the cheek.

"I love you, Percy Ford.

Chaotic or not, Percy acquired a few associates. So, when an opportunity came up in Delaware he jumped at the chance.

"But what will I do there? I love New York, and I have made some good friends here."

"I imagine you'll do that there too. Everybody is so friendly here; it won't take you long to fit it there too."

Percy had already secured lodgings and a first-class carriage, so was not about to be swayed.

"It'll be fine love. I promise."

Elsie smiled, nodded and began packing for Delaware.

The autumn leaves were beginning to change colour as they boarded the train bound for Delaware. There was a tear in Elsie's eye, and she was unusually quiet. Percy wondered if perhaps he'd been a little selfish and squeezed her hand reassuringly eye.

71

"Give it a chance love. If you really hate it, we can always go back."

"Thank you." She whispered.

"Oh, my word! Did you do all this for me?"

Percy nodded. He had the biggest smile on his face she'd ever seen.

"I don't know what to say."

"Do you like it?"

"Like it? I positively love it— you really are the best Percy Ford."

They were stood outside two shop fronts, which had once been a single, large shop. Unknown to Elsie, Percy had converted this into two units. One was Delaware Stationary, proprietor Mr P.T Ford. The other had the most beautiful sign which read "Elsie's Emporium" and was filled with beautiful fabrics, ribbons, and laces. Elsie hadn't wanted to leave New York but right now, it felt a small price to pay, in exchange for her own business.

That summer was perfect, they both worked hard—Elsie's dresses became the talk of the town. No self-respecting Senator's wife, or gangster's moll would be seen wearing anything else. Her slogan became "Would you dare to be seen in anything Elsie".

Percy too was happy and then it happened!

Percy returned home to find Elsie sat at the kitchen table with tears streaming down her face.

"What on Earth is the matter? You're not – well, you know? Not again, surely?"

Elsie nodded between sobs.

"But we've been so careful."

"I know but I've missed two now, so I know."

"Oh."

Percy took Elsie's hand.

"We must return to England and find parents. Besides, we've been fortunate here, we have a tidy sum put by, so we can return as comfortably as we arrived. There is one thing I want to do though, before we leave."

"What's that?" Elsie peered up into Percy's eyes, as she dabbed her own with a handkerchief.

"Marry you of course. I'll be damned if I'm having another child born out of wedlock."

"But Percy, you're already married—to Daisy—remember?"

"I know that, and you know that but nobody else here knows that do they?"

"Well, no, but... but it's illegal... Immoral even. We'd never get away with it... would we?"

"Sure, we would, whose to know except us?"

"Well, if you're sure?

"I'm absolutely sure. It would be our secret. And this baby would at least have wedded parents."

"Then yes. Yes. Absolutely yes!"

"Then that's settled. Get your coat Elsie. There's no time like the present."

Within hours Elsie Simmonds, became Elsie Ford, and both shops, along with the apartment upstairs were up for sale.

It was several months later, on a cold February morning that they stepped foot aboard the ship bound for home as Mr and Mrs Percy ford.

Elsie was several months pregnant by the time they set sail for England.

The crossing seemed long and arduous, cold weather and rough seas slowed the passage and Elsie struggled between morning sickness and seasickness. Percy too battled with his own seasickness, which was even worse than it had been on the journey to America.

Eventually, they arrived back in Southampton as Mr. Percy Ford and Miss Elsie Simmonds. They both knew their wedding was something that could only ever be their secret. Percy squeezed Elsie's hand, and whispered softly as they stepped off the gangplank.

"Come on Mrs. Ford, let's find somewhere warm to get some food and a bed for the night. We can sort out some lodgings tomorrow. I don't think I could go another day without a decent night's sleep."

They found a half decent board and lodgings for the night, and both were asleep as soon as their heads hit the pillow.

JUNE 1912

Percy and Elsie stayed in lodgings until the baby arrived. However, Percy made a couple of trips home to visit Daisy and Jack.

The first of these visits was primarily to inform Daisy of the current state of affairs.

"Jesus, Percy, can't you keep your hands off her for 5 minutes? And is Elsie so dim-witted, she can't work out her times?"

"That's enough Daisy! Keep a civil tongue in your head."

"Well, honestly? Another bastard child? You can sort this one out yourself Percy Ford. I wash my hands of the pair of you."

Percy returned to Elsie, quite despondent.

"The woman's a viper." Elsie snapped. Her response was to be expected, there was no love lost between the two women. Daisy was tired of Elsie's unending stream of pregnancies and Elsie was tired of Daisy's acid tongue.

"That Daisy is a selfish, dispassionate Bobtail. I swear it's more through luck than judgement that she hasn't contracted the 'lady's fever' ... although, who would know if she had, it may just be in its early stages." Percy nodded but was more concerned with the matter in hand, and as much as he disliked Daisy, this was no solution to their immediate problem.

The next time Percy returned to the Island was to visit Reginald and Georgina, in the hope that they might accommodate another of his and Elsie's 'mishaps.' Fortunately, this visit went better than the one to Daisy.

"Of course, of course, old man. We'd be more than happy to help, wouldn't we Georgie?"

"Absolutely, Percy and Alfred are such delights. We feel positively blessed."

Percy smiled, he was happy that his children were so well cared for. He knew Elsie would too. Reginald and Georgina were the height of discretion too. He and Elsie couldn't have asked for more.

Elsie, and Percy handed their newborn baby boy to Georgina on the 10th of November 1912.

"I'd like to call him Laurence," Georgina announced passing the baby to Reginald. "But," she added taking Elsie's hand, "I feel that his middle name should be Simmonds after his mother. After all dear, you have given us so much. Three darling boys, when we had been trying so long for just one. You are a treasure Elsie, you both are." Elsie smiled, squeezed Georgina's hand, and managed a weak 'thank you' as tears began to form.

"Thank you both." Reginald managed, taking Elsie's hand. The journey home was mostly quiet, but the silence was eventually broken.

"I know the boys are well cared for, but do you ever think about ... you know ... our first child?"

"Our daughter? Of course, I do, why?"

"I think I'd like to know how she is—wouldn't you?"

"I suppose so. I try not to think about it too much. Perhaps I'll ask Daisy, when things are a little calmer between us." Elsie hugged him, and even managed a weak laugh.

"Good luck Percy Ford, I reckon we'll be grandparents before that happens."

"I reckon you're right Else," he smiled.

It was the first time they had laughed for a while.

"You'll be thrilled to know that the Socialist party have included your lot in their manifesto. They won't be voted into power then."

Daisy plonked the paper down, but it hardly hit the table before Elsie grabbed it.

"I can't believe it; this is the most positive thing yet ..."

"It's only because your lot paid them. They wouldn't otherwise."

"You're wrong Daisy, I believe the National Union of Women's

Suffrage Societies, made a donation, but that's all."

"The National Union of Women's Suffrage Societies, Lord help us," Daisy scoffed, as though it left a nasty taste in her mouth. "Like I said your lot bought them."

"That's enough." Percy butted in, secretly squeezing Elsie's leg under the table. "Well done love," he mouthed winking at her.

Daisy threw him a look, which both he and Elsie ignored.

CHRISTMAS 1913

Christmas in the Welton, Simmonds, Ford household had largely consisted of Daisy's Uncle Charles coming to the island for the festivities. This meant he descended on Percy and Daisy, while Elsie was expected to cook and clean. It wasn't until later that Elsie and Percy exchanged gifts. Elsie hated Christmas; it was a lavish affair for everyone in the house except her. Percy hated it for exactly the same reason.

This year however, things would be different. Daisy's uncle had been taken ill, in the November, and Daisy and Jack had returned to London to help with his care, leaving Elsie and Percy alone. The Bath House was closed for a couple of days, so they took the opportunity to have a proper Christmas, and of course, New Year.

"To absent, drunken bobtails."

"Oh Elsie." Percy laughed, "it's a good thing she can't hear you."

"I wouldn't say it if she could, now, would I?"

"I guess not. Y'know Else this is just what we needed. It's been difficult, these last few months since we returned. And just think, for these short weeks we get to be Mr and Mrs P Ford, even if it is only behind closed doors."

"I love you, Percy."

Those few weeks flew by, and Daisy eventually returned mid-January.

"So where is she then?"

"On the mainland, there is a suffragette rally."

"Well, with any luck she'll get arrested and die on hunger strike."

"That's an awful thing to say Daisy Welton, you take that back."

"I will not! My uncle says I should never have agreed to her being here. If nothing else, her being here takes your attention away from Jack."

"Ah, now I get what it's about. You saw Jack Skipton, and he either bedded you or ignored you, but either way he doesn't want you, or Jack."

Daisy sat down and sighed. Percy was right. She had indeed come across Jack while on the mainland and their brief encounter hadn't gone how she had hoped.

"He's a pig, always was Daisy, you know that. If he was any sort of a man, he'd have married you years ago. Don't take it out on Elsie though, she has always been nice to our Jack."

"I know, and I am sorry. I just wish someone loved me, the way you love Elsie."

"You wish Jack Skipton loved you, and he's too selfish to love anyone. You had a lucky escape if you ask me ..."

"... I didn't." Percy ignored the interruption. "... as I was saying, you'll find someone one day. I'm sure of it."

There was no official suffragette rally in January 1913,

but there was a meeting, which however peaceful resulted in several arrests, including Elsie's. It seemed the authorities were growing increasingly less tolerant. This time however, they were released quite early. The rumour was that Emmeline Pankhurst's husband, brother, or possibly even Emmeline herself paid their fines.

Elsie returned home on January 30th, a little thinner for a few days hunger strike, but suffering no real ill effects.

"At least this time they didn't try force feeding us."

Daisy and Percy both winced at the thought.

"I'm just glad you're alright." Percy managed as Daisy passed her a cup of tea.

"One of the suffragettes, a friend, Kathleen Smith, says we are on the brink of a war. She said Emily had had her fortune told."

Percy looked sceptical, but Daisy gestured for her to continue.

"Apparently, this fortune teller, told her, Emily, that there would be a great war but that she wouldn't live to see it."

"Emily? *Emily*?" He thought he should probably know her name, but he didn't recall her having mentioned it.

"Emily Davison, she is very close to Emmeline Pankhurst."

"Well, that doesn't take a genius, or any sort of mysticism, these women are forever on hunger strike. You can't keep doing that, it's bound to take its toll. And from what I've heard Emily Davison is worse than most."

"Daisy's right love, look how thin you look after only a few days."

"Well, maybe. But what if she's right about the war?"

"I hope she isn't."

Daisy and Elsie nodded.

"I have to go back in April, war or no war, something big is happening in the movement, I can feel it."

"Let's hope you stay out of trouble, whatever it is. I can't deal with Percy moping around while you starve in prison."

As it happened neither Percy, nor Daisy needed to be concerned as the meeting in April came and went uneventfully. At least no one was arrested.

Percy greeted Elsie as she stepped off the ferry.

"So, how was the meeting. Is something big happening?"

"Oh, Percy it is something very big, very, very big." Elsie beamed. "It will be starting in June and end in July in Hyde Park. It will be the biggest gathering of suffragettes, ever. Isn't it exciting?"

"It certainly is, and I wish you all the best of luck."

Daisy was not so welcoming. She took one look at Elsie as she took her coat off.

"So, when's this one due Elsie."

Percy and Elsie both scowled at her.

"Hello, to you too Daisy."

"Does he know?" Daisy nodded toward Percy. "Well? Does he?"

"Yes, I know!" snapped Percy. "For a change, I knew before you Daisy Welton."

"So, when does it arrive?"

"Around November time, but we might be keeping this one. I'm hopeful the rally in July will go well."

"It's about time, I mean, I wondered how long this would go on for. You're like a damn breeding mare."

Life was good, Elsie felt certain the rally would go well for them. She also felt sure that although the newly formed Labour party had lost the last election, they would win the next.

By the end of May, Elsie was almost totally preoccupied with her preparations for the march to Hyde Park. She had washed her dress and sash ready for the occasion. Then on the 5th of June 1913 news reached the Isle of Wight of the tragic death of Emily Davison.

Percy came home to a distraught and completely inconsolable Elsie. Elsie's tears streamed down her face as she told Percy and Daisy about the great Emily Davison.

"I only met her a couple of times, once in prison, back in January... She was on hunger strike ... we all were, but there was something about her. She was fearless ... far braver than the rest of us. The second time I met her was in April... with Kathleen, when she confided in me that she'd seen that fortune teller... You know the one I told you about. I'm not sure Emily believed it, but Kathleen did. Remember, the one who told her about the war." Elsie paused, before almost whispering, "If the fortune teller was right about her death, you don't think she could've been right about ... you know..." She dropped her voice further "... the war."

"Certainly not," snapped Daisy. "I've never heard such poppycock. You need to get these silly ideas out of your head, especially if you are going to be a mother."

The word crashed through her ears. "Mother."

She'd almost forgotten about that. She needed to address that sooner rather than later.

"I can't do this—I can't be a mother, I'm not ready to be, I have too much to do."

"The first thing you need to do is get some rest," Percy whispered, tucking her in, and kissing her on the forehead. "I love you and we will work something out."

She managed a weak "I love you too," before falling asleep.

The conversation with Daisy the following morning didn't go so well.

"Really, Elsie, another one up for the scrap heap." Daisy piped up, before taking another mouthful. "I'm beginning to wonder if you have an ounce of compassion in you—certainly precious little in the way of maternal instinct."

"Whereas you are all heart."

Daisy stood up, both hands firmly on the table. She had a penchant for the dramatic if nothing else.

"I'm going before I say something we all regret."

She tossed her head with a final harrumph before leaving the room, dragging Jack behind her.

Elsie shook her head in dismay, Percy on the other hand was his usual reassuring self.

"We'll find someone to have the baby, and you can get back to London, and get that bloody vote for women. I never thought I'd say it but the longer I live in this house, the more I think women need more rights."

Daisy came home to Elsie delivering her 5th child. Percy was pacing up and down the hall, while the midwife, a suffragette ally was in attendance.

"How long has she been in there Percy?"

"Only about 10 minutes, or so why?"

Daisy didn't get a chance to reply, as no sooner had Percy closed his mouth than the first cries of his youngest daughter could be heard.

"Thank the Lord, that was mercifully quick."

"I'm surprised it took that long," Daisy sneered. "I mean ..."

Percy scowled at her, she shrugged, and opened her mouth to continue.

"Daisy Ford don't you bloody dare, you can keep your vile comments to yourself." She knew he meant it. He only ever called her Ford when he was in a rage with her, the rest of the time she was Daisy Welton. Calling her Ford was his way of reminding her that she was still his wife, and as such should do as her husband said.

She glared at him.

"I'm telling you Daisy, keep a civil tongue in your mouth or you'll be out on the street."

She didn't think he meant that. Percy wasn't the type to throw anyone out on the street but just in case, she decided to keep her thoughts to herself.

"Are you sure about this, they will wait till after Christmas. I mean they're not going anywhere."

"I'd rather get it over with and get back to some sort of normality."

"Well, if you're sure."

"Yes I am."

Percy held her hand when the new parents arrived at the bath house.

"We've registered the birth, so she knows where she's from and if you wouldn't mind, we'd like you to tell her why we were unable to keep her."

Elsie nodded before adding to the conversation.

"I wanted to keep her, but I believe it is important that little girls like her have a better world to live in."

"Is her name still Gwendolyn Olive like we agreed?"

Elsie nodded proudly, wiping a tear from her eye, as she handed her daughter to the new mum. The woman was beaming, and her eyes shone with delight as she looked at the little bundle.

"Thank you, and merry Christmas."

Both women giggled and the new mum smiled softly, before whispering, "you keep fighting for our future now, you hear me. You're brave lasses, the lot of you. Don't you dare quit."

"I won't." Elsie reassured her, planting a goodbye kiss on Gwendolyn's forehead.

Percy and the new dad did little more than exchange a few pleasantries throughout the whole thing.

"She'll be fine Else," he said taking her hand. "She'll know how brave her mother was, and she'll love you for it."

They spent Christmas that year blissfully unaware that by this time the following year they would at war.

A WORLD WAR

It was early one morning, when Percy picked up the morning paper and unfolded it.

"Heir to the Austrian Throne and his Wife Shot Dead in Street at Serajevo after Bomb had Failed." He announced. Percy had taken to announcing the headlines a few months previous, in an attempt to prevent Daisy and Elsie just bitching at each other. So far it had worked.

"It would appear that two deliberate, cold-blooded attempts, on the heir's life were made." Percy continued, following a dramatic pause.

"But why?" Elsie asked, but both women looked equally confused.

"I don't know. It doesn't say."

"I expect it's political" Daisy interjected. "It's always political. Perhaps it'll start Elsie's war, the one the fortune teller told her friend about."

Elsie scowled, and Percy rolled his eyes, and quickly continued.

"It says the Duchess was killed trying to shield her husband."

'Not much danger of that in this house.' Percy thought to himself. 'They'd be too busy killing each other, to protect me.'

"I wouldn't write Elsie's war off just yet." Percy continued. "It says here, on page 3, that war has been declared as a result."

"What war. Give me that." Daisy grabbed the paper and turned rapidly to page 3.

"Well, what does it say?"

"It says" Daisy directed the conversation at Elsie, having taken charge of Percy's morning paper. "Declaration of War by Austria-Hungary on Servia. It also says it's a 'Terrible Danger' that threatens Europe."

The colour drained from Elsie's face. She may have had slightly more faith in the fortune teller than the others, but she hadn't really expected there to be a war.

Over the coming days, the talk among the regular customers of the bathhouse seemed solely focused on war. It was, for the most part, speculative.

"They are such brave boys."

"Our fearless lads in the rifles."

"Them nippers'll show the Germans what's what."

All gossip aside, even Daisy had noticed there was a lot of activity involving the Isle of Wight Rifles.

And sure enough, only a few days later, Percy read the chilling "breakfast" headline.

"Great Britain Declares War on Germany."

Breakfast was silent that morning.

Britain had only been at war a matter of weeks when Daisy decided it was time to address the elephant in the room.

"So, Elsie Simmonds, exactly when are you planning on telling us about this baby?"

The table fell silent.

Percy unfolded the paper in the hope of salvaging a more peaceful breakfast.

"Don't you dare Percy Ford. Don't you dare!!" Daisy barked. "If you think you are going to brush this under the carpet you are very much mistaken."

"I'm not sure what business this is of yours Daisy Welton. But if you must know we are keeping this one."

"You're keeping it?"

"My baby is not an it."

With that Elsie left the room, tears streaming down her face.

"Are you happy now Daisy?" Percy growled.

"I'd be happier if she left. Honestly Percy, what is it with you? Can you really not keep your hands off each other. And call yourself a man? She walks all over you—you're a simpering fool with no backbone. I don't know why my uncle thought you'd make a decent husband. I mean-"

"ENOUGH!!" Jack who had been sat quietly at the table throughout this and many other heated breakfasts, had had enough.

"Just stop it Mother. All you ever do is shout at people or make snide digs at them. Elsie's done nothing to you, and she's always been nice enough to me. And what's Dad ever done except try and do right by all of us, and all you ever do is bitch and moan at everyone."

Daisy landed a well-aimed cuff to Jack's head.

"How dare you. How dare you speak to me like that. I am your mother!"

"I hate you!" Jack screamed repeatedly holding his face, as he stood up, kicked the chair and stormed out.

Percy rushed after him.

"You really are a selfish, bitter woman at times Daisy Welton."

Within minutes of leaving the room, Elsie, Percy and Jack all reappeared with luggage.

"We're off now Daisy. We will be staying at the cottage on the mainland and Jack's coming with us for a bit. It's safer there."

Safer? From what? Her or the war? Was she really such an awful person?

Daisy nodded contrite. It seemed the war was everywhere, including her own parlour.

The family returned at Christmas, to what they hoped would be a peaceful reunion. Daisy had written many lengthy and profusely apologetic letters to all of them, both individually and as a collective. Percy at least was optimistic that she had seen the error of her ways.

Daisy had prepared supper and did seem to be making an effort to be more accommodating. Elsie, who was heavily pregnant, retired early and Jack, still wary of his mother, likewise took the opportunity to excuse himself early.

Percy could tell by the look on her face something was bothering her.

"It's been a long day, the nipper's just tired—he'll be right as rain tomorrow you'll see."

"It's not that Percy, although that is something else of course, and I'm sure you're right."

"Then what is it?"

"I know, you never meant for this to happen, and I also know that I played a big part in everything, and for that I'm sorry. I also know that I have been very difficult, at times downright horrible to Elsie, and I'm sorry for that too." Percy opened his mouth to speak but Daisy threw him a look and he thought better of it. "It's been difficult. People round here aren't blind nor are they stupid, and unfortunately, they aren't quiet either. They might talk in hushed tones, but I'm not deaf and I hear what they say about us—about me. I'm a laughing stock—I know that. People round here think I'm a weak and foolish woman, who is nothing more than a maid to my husband and his mistress."

"Oh, I see. I never realised ..."

"...I know, but there's more." She continued cutting Percy off in mid-sentence. She didn't want apologies and platitudes, she wanted assurance. "I need to know that when the baby arrives, you will still be a father to Jack. I mean, well, I know he's not yours, but he doesn't know his real father, and ..."

"Of course, I will." Percy was slightly irritated by the question. "Haven't I always been—why would that change?"

Daisy was quiet, she knew she had offended him and while that wasn't her intention, she had to concede that where Jack was concerned, she had no reason to doubt Percy.

"Would you prefer us to move out once the baby's born? I can see that it might be for the best."

"No Percy, there's no need, we'll work it out, underneath it all I like Elsie and so does Jack."

"What if we can't work it out? Then what?"

"Then I'll go."

It was a freezing cold, dark January morning when Muriel Elsie Ford came into the world.

"She's a beauty." Daisy beamed passing the babe to her mother. It had been a long labour and Daisy had been in attendance the whole time.

Daisy opened the door to find Percy still pacing up and down.

"Percy, you have a daughter, and she is rather lovely. Would you like to meet her?"

Percy didn't need asking twice he practically raced to Elsie's bedside.

"Muriel, meet your father."

"Has she got a middle name?

"Not yet, I thought you could choose that one."

"Well in that case she is Muriel Elsie – after her mother who I love very much."

"Aw Percy you old romantic."

"Come on lover-boy, let Muriel get some grub and Mum get some sleep." Daisy interrupted, quite embracing her role as nursemaid.

"We are a real family now," he whispered, kissing Elsie on the forehead.

War, or no war Percy was the happiest man alive.

KATHLEEN

"Oh Elsie, really? Again?" Percy looked up and peered from Daisy to Percy, who in turn threw knowing glances at each other.

"I think I'd like a brother this time." Jack added, with a mouthful of egg. Daisy glared at him.

"Manners Jack! We don't speak with a mouthful of food, do we?"
He shook his head sheepishly and swallowed his food.

"*But I really would like a brother this time.*"

Elsie smiled and tried hard not to laugh, but it was hopeless. Daisy too began to giggle leaving Percy to explain how that was something they had no control over.

"Oh, I know," said Jack. "But none of that stops me wanting one."

"Fair enough son," Percy smiled.

The sky hung low in the sky and a warm yellow autumn glow shone in through the window of the dining room. Jack was amusing his baby sister Muriel while Daisy, Percy and Elsie enjoyed a leisurely breakfast. The world may have been at war, but for the residents of Ventnor bathhouse life couldn't be better.

Percy and Daisy had both remained true to their words, Percy continued to be a good father to Jack and Daisy learned to bite her tongue—most of the time.

In the midst of this idyllic scene came a knock at the door. Elsie, in her guise as housekeeper, opened it, returning a couple of minutes later with a letter, which she handed to Percy. There was no mistaking his mother's handwriting, the most perfect copper plate lettering gracefully swirled across the page. The writing may have been beautiful, the news, however, wasn't.

"What is it Perce?"

Elsie scowled at Daisy. How dare she be the first to ask that question, that was her place, and why did she insist on calling him Perce—his name was Percy.

Elsie leaned over and took his hand.

"Is everything alright *Percy*?"

"It's my father. He passed away last night. My mother found him this morning. I knew he'd been ill, but he was quite chipper when I saw him yesterday." The colour had drained from Percy's face and in his eyes, there was a far away, hauntingly empty expression.

Daisy quickly reached for the teapot and began pouring him a cup, while Elsie did her best to comfort him.

"Forgive me," he said, seeming to return his faculties. "I must go to my mother. She will need my assistance in making any necessary arrangements."

"Of course, we understand, don't we Daisy."

"Yes, yes, of course."

"And Percy, take all the time you need."

❖

"I'm so sorry." Daisy said fixing her funeral hatpin in place. Elsie shrugged.

"It's not your doing, so I shouldn't worry. Besides, it's a beautiful day, so I'll take Muriel out for a walk. I could do with some fresh air."

Percy's mother had made it very clear from the beginning that she did not, and would not, view Elsie as anything other than her son's, less than discreet dalliance. He was legally married to Daisy and that was that. If anything, Elsie was an embarrassment and a hindrance to her son's social standing.

Percy and Daisy could see the tears forming and Percy hugged her tight. Daisy bustled Jack out of the front door.

"We'll wait outside." She was more or less addressing herself. Percy and Elsie were attempting to console each other. Her trying to ease the pain of his loss, and him trying to reassure her that his opinion of Elsie was nothing like his mother's.

Elsie was already resigned to the fact that Christmas would no doubt involve inviting Percy's newly widowed mother. In truth, she knew that, with his dad gone, his mother had nothing else to focus upon. She also suspected that from now until her dying breath, his mother would make it her life's mission to rid her son of his *dreadful* concubine. Elsie dearly hoped Percy's mother would find something else to fill the void left by his father's passing.

"What's happening? Is my baby alright? Tell me Daisy? Please. Oh please, let my baby be alright."

Daisy held the tiny baby and delivered a slap to the blood-stained buttocks.

"It's a girl" squealed Daisy, as the previously silent baby screamed at the top of her lungs.

"And she's beautiful."

Daisy handed the small girl to Elsie. She was a little thing whose birth had been a long and at times traumatic event. Daisy had worried either mother or daughter may not make it but here they were, a bit battered and bruised, very tired but both alive and well.

Percy popped his head round the door. Daisy gestured to him to be quiet and get out. He ignored her. He felt, that having spent several hours pacing up and down the hallway, aware Elsie was struggling with this one, he had every right to see that they were both alright. Daisy tutted several times, but Percy continued to ignore her.

Elsie was asleep with a sleeping baby wrapped up on her chest. This one was much smaller than her siblings had been and as yet unwashed. Percy, however, thought it was the most glorious sight, his secret wife and tiny daughter were just perfect.

Life was perfect.

Percy had come to a difficult decision. Following the birth of his youngest daughter, who Elsie had named Kathleen after her friend in the suffragette movement. He had decided that his mother was no longer welcome in his house.

He'd be damned if his mother was coming for Christmas and spending the day bitching about his wonderful Elsie. They were his family, and he was proud of them whether his mother approved or not. His secret wife, Muriel, little Kathleen, and Jack was his family. Even Daisy was nicer to Elsie than his mother. Enough was enough.

Elsie's parents were no better, and she hadn't seen either of them since she was moved in with Percy. They viewed her in much the same way Percy's mother did. The bathhouse inhabitants may not have been the most conventional family, but they had found a way to make it work, and for the most part it did.

THE FORTUNE TELLER

"Oh Percy, she was wonderful. Emmeline is like a goddess, and her words have power. We have never been so close to achieving our goals … and Daisy, you should have seen it. There must've been a hundred women there. We may only have had a few brief moments, but they were inspirational moments."

Her eyes glazed over, and the smile faltered, her bottom lip trembling. Percy smiled, a kind and gentle smile.

"What is it love, what's wrong?" He was proud of Elsie. She was fighting for a better world. She may not have been drafted but she was a soldier, nonetheless.

"It's Kathleen, do you remember the girl I told you about. The one our Kathleen is named after. The one who told me about Emily and the fortune teller. Apparently, a few weeks ago Kathleen visited the same woman and was told that she wouldn't live to see us get the vote."

"Does this fortune teller ever say anything good?" Daisy snapped. "Why can't she see tall, dark, handsome strangers, happy marriages, health and good fortune, etcetera."

"I'm sure I don't know," replied Elsie. "What I do know, is that she was right about Emily and the war. I also know that Kathleen is my friend and has fought tirelessly for women's rights. We have all experienced being beaten by the police, brutal arrests, prison, and hunger strikes. Imagine, Daisy, going through all that and not seeing your goals achieved. It's too sad." She shook her head and her eyes watered slightly. "But ..." she paused and smiled at her children affectionately. "I believe *their* world will be a very different place to ours."

Daisy couldn't imagine any of that. In fact, while Daisy didn't necessarily embrace Elsie's 'antics' as she called them, she was quietly fascinated by the women's movement, and wondered what this world Elsie dreamed of would entail.

There was no way that she would ever have put herself through all that, being beaten, arrested, and going on hunger strike was not becoming to a lady. It was all far too undignified. However, she wasn't keen on rationing either, and even less keen, on the whole idea of women doing men's work. She wasn't sure whether Elsie's dream world would be any better. Mostly she thought it was just that—a dream world.

ALMOST A VICTORY

It was bitter cold February morning as Elsie crept tentatively out of bed. She had not been well. The cold winter had taken its toll, and this was the first night, in a few weeks that she had slept right through. She sat on the edge of the bed and breathed deeply, there was no rasping or urgency to cough. She had to admit she felt much better.

In the dining room Daisy and Percy were grinning from ear to ear and waving the papers at her.

She rubbed her eyes, to check she wasn't dreaming but there it was in black and white.

VOTERS INCREASED BY 8,000,000 MEN AND WOMEN

"It's good isn't it love. It means you've done it."

"It's a start but it's not the result we wanted."

"Why not?" Daisy asked. "It says we can vote in the next election, isn't that what you were all fighting for."

116

"But I can't vote, can I?

"Why ever not? It says you can, doesn't it."

"No Percy, it doesn't. It says Daisy can, but I can't. I'm a housekeeper, and as such not eligible. Do you see, all men over 21 can vote, but we have to be 30, and proprietors. It's a start, and above all it makes our goal more achievable."

"Who would you vote for?" Daisy piped up.

"Whoever I thought would be on our side and contributed to us getting equal voting rights. Ideally, I'd want to vote for someone who would improve women's working conditions. Honestly Daisy, you have no idea. I mean, some of the horror stories the girls tell at the London gatherings—simply awful..."

"I work" Daisy butted in indignantly. "I'll have you know I work really hard."

"Oh Daisy, you work here. I'm talking about the girls in the factories, laundries, and mills. The ones who start work at a young age. One of the girls told me how she was abused by the foreman from the age of 11."

"That's not even legal. I don't believe you!"

"I think that's the point Elsie is trying to make—don't you?"

Daisy scowled at Percy. He, in turn winced. Daisy had a scowl that could turn milk sour.

"It is, thank you Percy" Elsie glared at Daisy. At which point the doorbell rang and Elsie shifted to answer it, but Percy waved her to remain seated.

"It may only be a small victory, but it is a victory. I'll get it, you eat your breakfast."

Elsie smiled. He was right it was a victory. Percy was just grateful for two minutes respite. He wasn't sure the women in his house needed any more power.

He returned to the dining room a few moments later with a letter. Elsie and Daisy were still sniping at each other.

"It's for you Else." He hastily handed her the letter. The sniping ceased but Daisy cast one last look across the table, but Elsie was oblivious, having become intrigued by the letter she'd just been handed. She didn't recognise the handwriting, but the postmark said London. She knew several people there. It was nice handwriting, so none of the factory girls she knew. Eventually she opened it. It was from a woman named Alice.

Dearest Elsie,

It is with great sorrow that I write to inform you of the death of Kathleen. She had contracted influenza earlier this year and sadly passed away on the 2nd of February. Always in our hearts.

Alice

Elsie wondered how she would remember this day, as a victory or a tragedy.

"Please excuse me" she said.

As she closed the door behind her, the tears began to streak her face.

"Rest in peace Kathleen," she whispered laying a single white rose on Kathleens grave. It had a small headstone which bore her name, dates, and nothing else. Kathleen, like many others, had been weakened by police brutality and the prison hunger strikes. This small, barely marked patch in Highgate seemed so little for such a brave soldier.

The day of the election came and went, and Daisy assured Elsie that she had voted conservative. She didn't. In fact, she didn't vote at all. She was never going to vote, but while she had no interest in politics, she knew how important it was to Elsie that she did. She was neither blind nor heartless. She had seen the state that Elsie came home in; the bruises and the weight loss that all too often followed suffragette rallies. She had seen Elsie's tears for Emily Davison and Kathleen, so she lied, because in the end lying seemed the kinder thing to do.

DAISY AND STAN

"Hold on, hold on. I'm coming." It appeared Percy could yell all he wanted, the knocking was going to continue until he opened the door.

"Daisy, for the love of God. What on earth..."

"For goodness' sake, Percy just let me in." She charged past him tears streaming down her cheeks and headed for the drawing room where she plonked herself down in an armchair.

Percy was completely dumbfounded by Daisy's impromptu and emotional early morning visit.

Elsie, was somewhat more practical, appearing in the drawing room with a tea tray and a glass of brandy.

"Here this'll help," she said handing Daisy the brandy. Daisy drank it straight down, and Elsie gestured for Percy to fetch the bottle while she poured the tea.

"Now Daisy, for goodness' sake what has happened?"

"It's ... it's ...it's Stan. I found him this morning ...." She began to sob uncontrollably, and Elsie quickly poured another brandy, which Daisy also drank in one gulp.

"He's dead." she finally managed.

"But how? Why?"

Daisy had moved out in 1919 when Stan's wife died. Daisy had moved in with him as his housekeeper. Elsie of course, had pointed out the irony of this, at every available opportunity, but Daisy didn't care. Elsie could laugh all she wanted, she and Stan were happy, or had been up until now. It was obvious that Daisy loved Stan, perhaps not in the same way she had loved Jack Skipton, but she definitely loved him.

"He was just hanging there," she sobbed. "It was awful .... Just awful."

Percy handed her a handkerchief and she obliged.

"I didn't know where to go. I just had to get out of that house."

Elsie sent Kathleen to fetch Jack.

"Why would he do such a thing?"

"He was ill. The doctor said it was consumption."

"TB?"

"Yes TB, Elsie." Daisy was getting quite fractious, and Elsie and Percy both heaved a sigh of relief when Jack appeared.

He helped his mother to her feet and escorted her to the front door.

'Thank you both.' he mouthed as he helped her down the front steps.

By the time they reached Stan's house, his body had been taken to the undertakers.

Jack, agreed to move in with his mother until after Stan's funeral.

"Are you alright love?" Percy peered over his paper.

"I have a letter in this hand which states that my father has passed away, and in this hand, I have a letter telling me that Doris...

our Doris, was married last month and has moved to the mainland. I'm sure Percy I don't know whether to grieve for my father or be happy for our daughter. It's a lot to take in. I think I shall be happy for Doris, after all he has been no father these past years. Neither he nor my mother have even met our children, except unknowingly perhaps. No, I think the old bastard can rot wherever he is."

"Elsie! Such language," Percy laughed. "And at the breakfast table too."

"Percy, do you think that perhaps we should consider moving."

"Why, and where to?"

Percy had often considered moving, especially in the early days but he owned this place and felt he would have to offer some remuneration to Daisy if he sold it. The money had come from her family after all.

"I was thinking perhaps Winchester. I believe Jack is moving to Southampton with his mother, and I, or rather we, will miss him when he goes. He may not be a legal child of ours, but he is very much like a son to you, and I view him as family. Also, I thought the girls could attend school there. They have such wonderful opportunities there for education. I would hate Kathleen or Muriel to end up in service or worse."

"I don't think that would happen, but you make a good argument. So, I will give it some thought."

He took a mouthful of tea, almost draining the cup in one.

"There, I've thought, we'll move to the mainland. I'll go and find us accommodation and we'll spend Christmas as residents of Winchester."

Elsie leapt out of her seat, flung her arms around him, and planted several kisses on his cheek.

"Do you mean it? Oh, I love you Percy Ford and thank you, thank you, thank you. It is too exciting."

"Well, I think I could appoint a manager in the bathhouse instead of selling it. That would still bring us an income from it while I seek employment or investment—whichever presents itself first."

Daisy sat across from the solicitor. He was a foreboding individual, tall, well dressed, with spectacles rested towards the tip of his nose. Even sitting down, he was tall, and Daisy felt quite small in comparison.

She could clearly see, the document on the table in front of him was 'The Last Will and Testament of Stanley Horatio Pearson.'

"Well Mrs Ford." He finally ventured. His speech was slow and methodical. "It would appear that you are the sole beneficiary of Mr Pearson's estate."

"Oh, I see. Well, actually no I don't see. What exactly are you saying?"

"I am saying, Mrs Ford, that Stanley Horatio Pearson left everything he owned to you."

"Oh, and what exactly did he own." The solicitor rolled his eyes.

"You have inherited his house, to do with as you see fit. Likewise, his savings, which adds up to 5,438 pounds, 12 shillings, and fourpence. Now, if there is nothing else, I am a busy man."

"Of course, of course, thank you for your help."

"Good day Mrs Ford. Close the door on the way out please." The solicitor added as Daisy left in a daze.

Within a month Daisy had sold the house and left for London. She felt after all that she'd lost, the island no longer felt like home.

Jack did indeed follow his mother to Southampton, and Percy, Elsie, and their daughters, followed Jack and set up residence in Winchester.

THE VOTE

Percy didn't wait for Elsie to come downstairs, instead he went charging upstairs clutching the newspaper and yelling at the top of his voice.

"Good Lord Percy, whatever is it?" Elsie had almost leapt out of her skin when the bedroom door flew open to reveal Percy frantically waving the paper and still shouting.

"Elsie, Elsie, it's too exciting. Look! Look!"

He practically shoved the newspaper up her nose. She, on the other hand carefully unrolled it to reveal the headline:

EQUAL VOTING RIGHTS FOR WOMEN GRANTED

Elsie just stared at it, tears forming as she remembered the rallies, the suffering, the heartbreak but most of all, she remembered the women. Those who lost their lives and those whom she had kept in touch with. She knew that all those she had called comrade, all those she had fought with, and all those she had laughed and cried with would all be reading this with tears in their eyes too.

"You did it love. You and all those other brave women. You've created a better world for our girls. I'm so proud of you."

She smiled at him.

"We did, didn't we? We bloody well did it."

"Come on, get dressed. I'm taking you out for breakfast, lunch, and dinner!"

A few days later, a letter arrived. This time it was typed. It was a beautiful letter, which began with, 'my dearest Elsie.' The letter told of Emmeline Pankhurst's death and how proud she would have been. It also, perhaps more importantly, thanked her, Elsie, for her valuable contribution, within the suffragette movement. It was signed, with affection and gratitude, from C Pankhurst.

Percy could see the tears in her eyes and hugged her tight.

"You know love, you can win a thousand victories and suffer as many losses, but I will always love you. I always have and nothing will ever change that."

Daisy too, read the headlines, and while she may have had no political aspirations, she was grateful for some equal rights.

She had recently run into the long since widowed Jack Skipton, who despite his 'Jack the lad' younger days had done quite well for himself. Daisy knew it was ridiculous but one look at Jack Skipton and her heart turned somersaults. They hadn't seen each other in 24 years but there she was, right back there, reliving their last moments together. She could feel herself blushing but was unable to control it. She was still a good-looking woman for her age, and despite being no spring chicken was still quite eligible. Even more so now that she had money. Jack, of course had grown more distinguished with age, and for once had no intention of taking advantage of her, or at least not financially.

They looked at each other, both knowing something was being rekindled, something, that this time, would last forever.

"Ooh, Percy. You'll never believe this. There's a letter for you, and if I'm not mistaken it's from Daisy."

Percy took the letter, and a deep breath, or perhaps it was a sigh, before opening it.

"What does it say?" Elsie could only think of two reasons why Daisy might write. Either Jack was getting married, or someone had died. Although beyond Jack she couldn't think of anyone else's death in Daisy's circle that would be of relevance to Percy. She really hoped death wasn't the case.

"She says, she is filing for divorce."

"Really?"

"It says so here." Percy handed her the letter.

"Perhaps you won't be my secret wife for much longer." He smiled at Elsie.

"But while you are, I think I'll make the most of it." He grabbed her hand and pulled her close, before whisking her off her feet and carrying her upstairs.

Their divorce was granted a year later, exactly 26 years since Percy and Daisy's wedding day. Both of them were far happier with their divorce than they were with their wedding.

Percy spent the entire day grinning like a fool and referring to Elsie as the formerly secret Mrs Ford.

Daisy had received the letter granting their divorce, opened it, kissed it, and whispered, 'Thank you Elsie Simmonds.'

A HARD DECISION

Winchester had progressed through the war relatively unscathed, certainly by comparison to other cities. Percy however did not fare so well.

It had begun in 1945, there was no knowing what had caused it. It may have been the stress of rationing, curfews, and the imminent threat that war poses. It may equally have been his youngest daughter Kathleen's decision to emigrate to California with an American GI. It may simply have been old age. Whatever the cause Percy had become increasingly confused.

He no longer told Elsie he loved her. Most of the time he didn't seem to care much about her at all. Elsie struggled to cope and spent a lot of time crying and wishing the man she loved would return. He never did.

By December 1948 Percy had become prone to aggressive

outbursts and Elsie felt she was no longer able to take care of him.

The ambulance arrived and Percy was taken to hospital.

"Why am I here? He asked Elsie on one of her daily visits. Most times he was unaware of her presence, other times he thought she was someone else, but today was a good day.

"You're here to get better," she reassured him taking his hand and squeezing it gently.

"I love you secret Mrs Ford," he smiled. "I hope you know that nothing can change that." A tear rolled down her face, this illness could and did change that. How could he love someone he didn't recognise.

That was the last time she saw Percy, after that, all she saw was the shell he had become. He had been moved to a local nursing home, deemed unfit to return home.

Eventually she made the agonising decision to stop visiting him. It was too painful. Jack and Muriel had given up a long time ago, and who could blame them. The man they had called father had long since disappeared, and now it was her turn to walk away.

She stood in his bedroom doorway for a second, watching him, hoping for a last glimpse of Percy, something to make her change her mind. Something to give her hope. There was nothing. And so, it ended with a look. Not a look of passion, nor a look of desperate longing but a look, nonetheless.

"Goodbye, my love." she whispered as she closed the door.